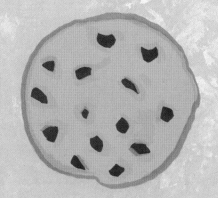

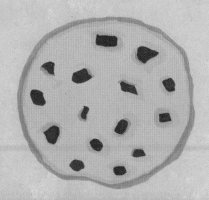
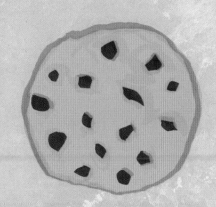
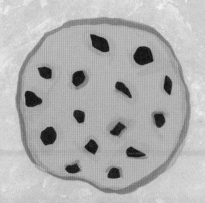
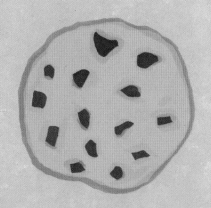
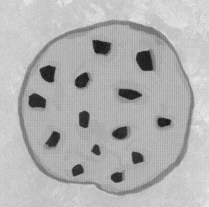
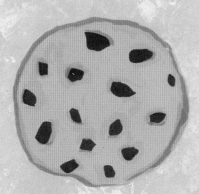

To my family, dinosaur fans,
and picky eaters

Henry Holt and Company, *Publishers since 1866*
Henry Holt® is a registered trademark of
Macmillan Publishing Group, LLC.
120 Broadway, New York, NY 10271 · mackids.com

Library of Congress Cataloging-in-Publication Data is available.
Our books may be purchased in bulk for promotional, educational, or business use.
Please contact your local bookseller or the Macmillan Corporate
and Premium Sales Department at (800) 221-7945 ext. 5442
or by email at MacmillanSpecialMarkets@macmillan.com.
First Edition, 2022
Printed in China by Hung Hing Off-set Printing Co. Ltd., Heshan City, Guangdong Province

ISBN 978-1-250-77996-0
10 9 8 7 6 5 4 3 2 1

I'm Hungry!
¡Tengo hambre!

Angela Dominguez

HENRY HOLT AND COMPANY
NEW YORK

Hiya!

Hola.

¡Tengo hambre!

Oh, you're hungry.

Well, what would
you like to eat?

You don't
know.

No se.

¿Plátano? No.

Fish?
They are
my favorite.

¿Pescado?
No, gracias.

How about lettuce?
Or a salad?

¿Lechuga o ensalada?

No.

Bread with some butter?
Everyone loves that.

¿Pan con
mantequilla? No.

Sigh.
I'll be back.

Sandwich?
¿Torta?

Cake?
¿Pastel?

Ice cream?
¿Helado?

Pizza?
¿Pizza?

¡No, gracias!

¿Un pajaro . . . ?

A bird?

¿ . . . azul?

Blue . . . ?

WAIT, WAIT!
A BLUE BIRD? NO!

COOKIES ARE MUCH BETTER.

Yes, I'm happy too!

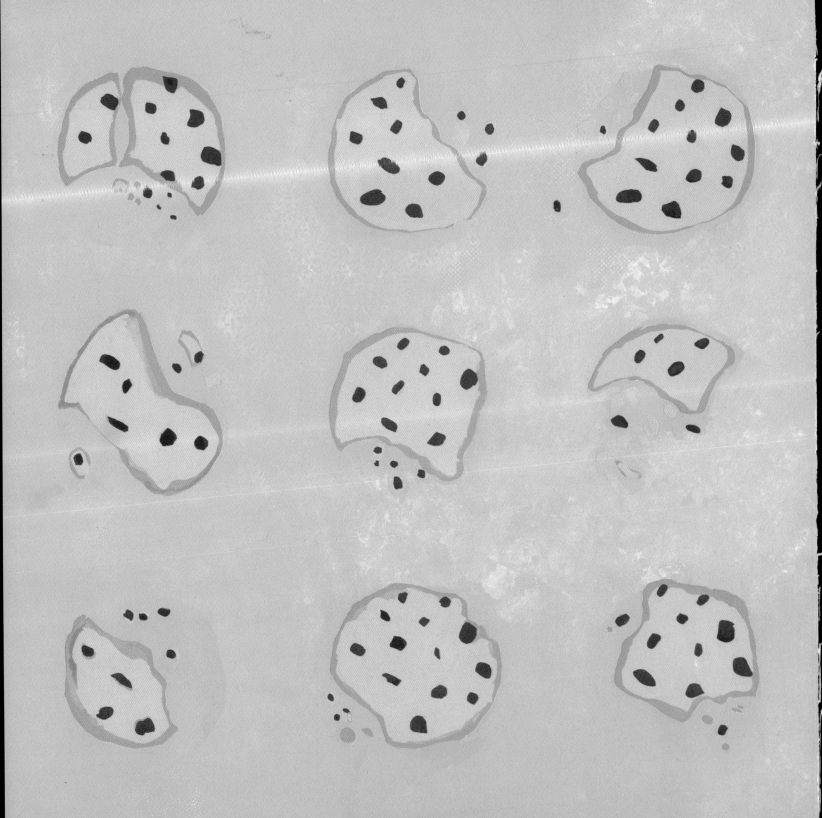